THE RAT WITH THE HUMAN FACE

THE QWIKPICK PAPERS

Books by Tom Angleberger

In the Qwikpick Papers series
Poop Fountain!
The Rat with the Human Face

In the Origami Yoda series
The Strange Case of Origami Yoda
Darth Paper Strikes Back
The Secret of the Fortune Wookiee
Art2-D2's Guide to Folding and Doodling
The Surprise Attack of Jabba the Puppett
Princess Labelmaker to the Rescue!
Emperor Pickletine Rides the Bus

Fake Mustache: Or, How Jodie O'Rodeo and Her Wonder Horse (and Some Nerdy Kid) Saved the U.S. Presidential Election from a Mad Genius Criminal Mastermind

Horton Halfpott: Or, The Fiendish Mystery of Smugwick Manor; Or, The Loosening of M'Lady Luggertuck's Corset

Amulet Books
New York

THE RAT WITH THE HUMAN FACE

THE QWIKPICK PAPERS

Found by
TOM ANGLEBERGER

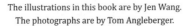

The illustrations in this book are by Jen Wang.
The photographs are by Tom Angleberger.

Library of Congress Cataloging-in-Publication Data

Angleberger, Tom.
The Rat with the Human Face / found by Tom Angleberger.
pages cm. — (The Qwikpick papers ; book 2)
Summary: While searching for the Rat with the Human Face, friendships fray as club members Dave and Lyle compete for Marilla.
ISBN 978-1-4197-1489-4
[1. Adventure and adventurers—Fiction. 2. Friendship—Fiction. 3. Clubs—Fiction. 4. Rats—Fiction. 5. Humorous stories.] I. Title.
PZ7.A585Rat 2015
[Fic]—dc23
2014038421

Printed and bound in U.S.A.
10 9 8 7 6 5 4 3 2 1

Amulet Books are available at special discounts when purchased in quantity for premiums and promotions as well as fundraising or educational use. Special editions can also be created to specification. For details, contact specialsales@abramsbooks.com or the address below.

THE ART OF BOOKS SINCE 1949
115 West 18th Street
New York, NY 10011
www.abramsbooks.com

For the Nerdy Book Club

An important note to the reader
from Tom Angleberger

This is the second of three stacks of papers this guy found in a storage room at the old Qwikpick gas station in Crickenburg. The guy, who asked me not to use his name, called me because one of my old newspaper articles was in the first stack. (You know I was a reporter before I wrote the Origami Yoda books, right?)

That article was about a sewage treatment plant and apparently it gave some kids the idea to sneak into the plant. If they had asked me, I would have told them not to because it is (a) dangerous and (b) stinks to high heaven.

Anyway, the kids—whose names are Lyle, Dave, and Marilla—actually went to see it and smell it. And they wrote a whole "Official Report" about it. Then they left the report at the Qwikpick and, after I got it, we published it under the name *The Qwikpick Papers: Poop Fountain!*

But here's the thing . . . that was just the FIRST official report on the stack. There were three. And this is the second one. I think we'll call this one: *The Qwikpick Papers: The Rat with the Human Face.* Why?

Well, because it's about a rat with a human face. Maybe. You'll have to read it to find out.

But before you read it, let me remind you that all this happened a long time ago. It was actually in the year 2000, and things were different back then. If these kids had had iPhones or smartphones like we do now, then their whole adventure would have been less dangerous. They would have downloaded flashlight apps onto their phones instead of stumbling around in the dark. And they could have called someone for help instead of being trapped in a disgusting basement . . . possibly forever.

But they didn't have phones. All they had was a watch and a camera. And even that camera isn't like the ones you have today. Those cameras took forever to charge the flash, they showed you your picture on a teeny tiny screen, and they drained batteries so fast it wasn't funny—or cheap. Plus they were about five times bigger and heavier than you'd think and the pictures were about 500 times worse.

So now you know what you need to know to read this "Official Report," but promise me you won't do anything this crazy yourself! I mean—these kids were a little bit nuts. And they're lucky they didn't starve, get rabies, or both.

But, if they had, they wouldn't have been able to produce this "Official Report" for us to read. And, even though I STILL haven't been able to track them down, I think they would be glad to know we're reading about their crazy adventure. So enjoy this, the second stack of crazy papers found by an anonymous dude at the Qwikpick . . . also known as *The Qwikpick Papers*.

Tom Angleberger

THE QWIKPICK PAPERS

The official report of The Qwikpick
Adventure Society's expedition to find the
Rat with the Human Face

The Qwikpick

SECTION I
Introduction

This is the semi-official report of The Qwikpick Adventure Society's Expedition to Find the Rat with the Human Face.

One reason it's only semi-official is because Lyle (me) has had to write it himself without Marilla and Dave. The reason why Marilla and Dave couldn't help is what this report is all about. Well, it's also about the Rat with the Human Face, of course.

Hopefully, after it's all typed up, I will be able to give Marilla and Dave a copy and see if they approve. That will have to be totally top secret, of course, since The Qwikpick Adventure Society has been officially banned. We're not even allo wed to meet at the Qwikpick--the convenience store where my parents work and Marilla, Dave, and me used to hang out.

(Dave had to do the drawings in secret and Marilla had to secretly give me the card from her digital camera to take to Walgreens to get the pictures printed out.)

So the report is semi-official because officially there is no Qwikpick Adventure Society. All because of the Rat with the Human Face. Frankly, I almost wish I had never heard of the Rat with the Human Face. He (or she) has caused nothing but trouble. But then again, maybe it was worth it since not many people ever get to see a Rat with a Human Face, not even in a zoo. It's hard to decide.

When I look back at the official report of our first trip (see: The Official Report of The Qwikpick Adventure Society's Trip to See the Fountain of Poop), I know that was one of the best days of all time. This rat trip was a little more complicated. There's some stuff that was good and some stuff that was the worst. But I'm going to write it all up anyway just to make sure that all the facts are put down and the real story is told.

And of course, the reason it is
typed on a typewriter is that I STILL
DON'T HAVE A COMPUTER! But I do
have this typewriter, which I got for
Christmas and which I've set up in
the break room at the Qwikpick, which
is whe re my parents work and where
we got the name for our club back
before it was banned.

UNOFFICIAL Personal Note

Don't worry. Not everything is as bad as that sounds. There's actually something completely great, but it can't go in the semi-official report. Even in a semi-official and top secret report there are things that are too unofficial and too top secret to put in. This story has a lot of those things. Dave and Marilla are my best friends, but there's no way I could tell them all the things that need to go into the full report. So I'm adding these comments to my copy so that the whole truth is recorded, even though I'm the only one who will ever read it. (Plus, sometimes I just think of something I forgot to put in and I don't want to have to retype a whole page just to add a sentence.)

Basically, what's going on is that my best friends, Dave and Marilla, are not allowed to hang out with me anymore and Marilla's parents actually want to move out of the Crab Creek Estates Trailer Park, where we both live, because of "bad influences," which basically means me, I guess, and maybe the guy in the trailer next to Marilla's who plays loud music and has lots of ladies over. But I think it mostly means me.

It's crazy that they think I'm a bad kid. I'm afraid of bad kids. It was a bad kid who threw my calculator onto the roof of the school. It was a bad kid who tore up my field trip permission slip so I almost didn't get to go to Monticello. And another one who got a worm while we were outside for PE, then took it back to math class and cut it up and secretly flicked the pieces at people, including the teacher.

My dad says that when you live in a trailer park some people will think you're a bad kid real easily. But I wouldn't have thought that Marilla's parents would look down on me for living in a trailer park, because they live in the SAME TRAILER PARK AS ME! But they're only there because Marilla's dad is real sick.

It's not my fault that I live in a trailer. It's all because of what my parents owe on their credit cards, is what my mom says. How does that make me more of a bad kid than Dave?

But Marilla is still allowed to eat lunch with Dave, but not with me. You call that fair? Of course, there's a little more to it, but I'll get to that later.

Basically, I'm just trying to say, what's wrong with living in a trailer? Nothing! Well, there are a few things that aren't so great about it, but I mean there's nothing wrong with a person who lives in a trailer.

Well, anyway, without Marilla and Dave, my life is really, really boring. It was so much fun when they would hang out with me at the Qwikpick after school, and now they're not even allowed to come here at all. So I'm either stuck here or at my trailer and I don't have any other friends and everything is a total, total disaster.

Except for one thing. There's one thing that's so, so good that it makes up for a lot of the lousy stuff.

And that is the other thing that this report is about and the main reason for writing secret notes that Marilla and Dave won't see. Because the really wonderful thing is about me and Marilla!!!!!

SECTION II
The Members of the Qwikpick Adventure Society

There are still just the three of us in the society. (Or we were in it, before it was banned.)

Marilla Anderson: Haiku superstar, current Ms. Pac-Man record holder, saxophone player, babysitter. Tall. ← *And very cute!*

Dave H. Raskin: Artist, reigning penny basketball champion, origami expert, trumpet player. Short.

Lyle Hertzog (me): Speed typist, future reporter (I hope), the rightful penny basketball champion if there was any justice!! Just slightly shorter than Dave.

For some reason, we offered to let Marilla's friend Elizabeth join the society, but when she found out we were going to look for a rat she said, "No thanks." It's probably a good thing we didn't tell her that our first trip was to see poop. (For more information, see The Official Report of The

Qwikpick Adventure Society's Trip
to See the Fountain of Poop.) I don't
think she really understood the point
of being in The Qwikpick Adventure
Society.

Dave and Marilla have been friends
for a long time. Lyle (me) started
eating lunch with them about a year
ago.

We all eat lunch at the nerd table,
which I guess means that we are all
nerds.

UNOFFICIAL Personal Note

I think Marilla is too pretty to be a nerd. But she eats at the nerd table anyway.

Dave and I definitely look like nerds. He doesn't seem to mind, but I do, and for a while I tried to look more normal by putting gel in my hair and wearing jeans. But Dave said the gel made me look like worse than a nerd and Elizabeth told me that my jeans were the wrong kind of jeans.

Anyway, most of the people at the table are in band, including Dave and Marilla. Which means they go on extra field trips and stay after school a lot practicing for the big Spring Concert. I'm in Rotation, which means instead of band I have a bunch of dinky classes that never take extra field trips, stay after school, or have Spring Concerts.

Basically, at the time that this story got started I was already sick to death of hearing about the Spring Concert. It was the only thing Marilla and Dave and the rest ever talked about.

Well, I guess it wasn't the only thing, but it sure got annoying hearing about who was going to dance while the band played "Boot Scootin' Boogie" or who would get to do the solo on "Totally Awesome Dinosaur Romp."

Anyway, the real reason it bugged me is that my number-one worry has always been that Dave might like Marilla too. So how was I supposed to compete with him when he got to spend all that extra time with her and then even when I was with them they spent half the time talking about band?

Geez, if I had realized that being in band was so important, I would have signed up for it.

Actually, the reason I didn't sign up for it was that the day the band teacher came to talk about signing up for band, I had gotten in trouble. Carrie Felman had said something and I said something back and the teacher acted like we were fighting and sent us to the office and by the time we got back the band teacher had come and gone and now Carrie and I are stuck in Rotation together forever and ever.

SECTION III
The Guy Who Saw the Rat

This story all began back when The Qwikpick Adventure Society had not been banned.

Strangely, the whole thing started on a Friday morning at the Qwikpick. The reason that's strange is that we're almost never at the Qwikpick in the morning.

On weekday mornings we're in school, of course. On Saturdays, Dave's family--which is Jewish--goes to synagogue and Marilla's family--which is Jehovah's Witnesses--goes around to people's houses to tell them about God. Then on Sundays Marilla's family goes to church.

However, the Qwikpick is a great place to be in the morning. So when we have a day off from school, Dave and Marilla usually meet me here early for breakfast. The Qwikpick serves a great breakfast. You can have all kinds of different biscuits--sausage,

egg, BLT, cheese, the Bilbo Baggins
Special, which is fried baloney,
and, best of all, gravy and biscuits.
If it looks like there's going to be
leftovers, Larry--who is the manager
and my parents' boss and a really nice
guy--gives them to us for free.

So on Lee-Jackson Day, which is
always on a Friday, we were all here
having breakfast. Why we have a holiday
for Lee and Jackson, who were Civil War
people who fought for the South, is a
good question and Marilla got an A for
an essay she wrote about why we should
get rid of it. But anyway, we have it,
and there we were eating breakfast.

Every morning, whether it's Lee-
Jackson Day or not, the Qwikpick is
crowded with construction workers
eating breakfast. See, there are
new houses being built all over
Crickenburg, especially in the old cow
fields back behind the Qwikpick and the
Crab Creek Estates Trailer Park.

So there are all these builders and
plumbers and electricians and truck

drivers and bulldozer people who stop
at the Qwikpick for coffee and biscuits
before they get started. That's why
my dad has to get up so early in the
morning to start making biscuits,
which he hates. (Both the getting up
early and the making biscuits.)

Most of them take their biscuits away
in to-go boxes, but some of them sit at
the tables along the front windows and
eat. We sit at these tables all the time
too, either for eating, homework, or
penny basketball purposes.

So that's how we heard the guy who
saw the rat tell his friends about it.
Obviously, I can't remember every word
he said, but this is as close as I can
get:

"Did I tell you guys about this
crappy basement job I was doing up at
Mount Perrin?"

"You mean the hotel?" asked one of
his buddies.

"No, the research station up there.
It's on past the hotel. They got this
huge old building up there for

scientists. They had me doing some wiring and stuff, then they asked me to redo the lights in the basement.

"This was the worst basement I've ever seen. Old junk everywhere and weird crap floating in bottles. That was some jacked-up stuff, man, and it stank. I think they used to keep animals down there and never cleaned it up. The wiring must have been a hundred years old. Big job to replace it all. I told them that.

"So I've got the power cut and it's pitch dark down there and I've got the flashlight in my teeth while I'm fishing some ten-gauge wire through the wall.

"That's when I hear something big moving around. I shined my light over to the doorway, and there is the biggest rat I've ever seen.

"He's just strolling by and then he stops and turns to look at me. And I swear to God that rat had a human face."

SECTION IV
A Unanimous Decision

The guy's buddies seemed to be only mildly impressed by his story, but not us. We were blown away.

For a long time we had wondered what our next adventure would be. What could possibly measure up to the Fountain of Poop? We had come up with lots of ideas, but they all seemed pretty dull compared to the poop fountain. We were getting desperate to get out and have another adventure.

Marilla looked at me and Dave and we all knew that this was going to be it--we had to see the Rat with the Human Face for ourselves.

We went upstairs to the Qwikpick break room to talk about it.

Basically, we're the only ones who actually use the break room, since you're not allowed to smoke in here and all the employees smoke so they go out back on their breaks. So Larry lets us keep it however we want. There's a lot of leftover stuff from when Larry used to live in the upstairs. There's an old sofa and an old recliner that someone in the trailer park gave us. Mostly, we sit around and watch old movies on a semi-working VCR, and channel seven, which is the only TV station we can get.

But it's also a great place to have official meetings and make secret plans.

"We're definitely going to do this, right?" asked Marilla. Dave and I both agreed immediately. Not only did we want to see the rat, but nobody wanted to be left out if the other two did something good.

"I wonder what it looks like," I said. "Maybe it's got some sort of mutation."

"Maybe it's a rat that got loose from an experiment up there and it's really smart," said Marilla.

"Actually," said Dave, "it's probably just a regular rat that's a little weird-looking, but I agree we should go see it. However, it's not going to be easy. For starters, how do we get there? I went up to the Mount Perrin Hotel with my family once and it was like almost an hour to get there. Plus, it's on top of a mountain, so there's no possible way we could ride our bikes up there."

"Maybe we can get someone to drive us," said Marilla.

But we all agreed that it seemed pretty unlikely that any of our parents would willingly drive us all that way to look for a rat. Plus, that wouldn't really be much fun.

"Maybe Larry would take us," I said.

"I seriously doubt that my parents would let me go anywhere with Larry," said Marilla.

"Same here," said Dave.

"Yeah, me neither," I admitted.

We sat around for a while and thought about it and didn't think of a way to get up there. So we decided to go outside and play

Larry is a super-nice guy, but my dad thinks he drinks too much.

our game of throwing a ball between the Dumpster and the Qwikpick without touching either one.

We played the Dumpster game until we got cold, then we watched a movie--<u>Better Off Dead</u>--our current favorite movie from the box of leftover videos from when the Qwikpick used to rent videos.

Then we went to look at the crane game. At first we hated the crane game, because it had replaced Ms. Pac-Man. Larry said he would much rather have Ms. Pac-Man than the crane game but the people at Qwikpick headquarters made him change it because crane games make a lot more money than video games. This was especially true since Larry had fixed Ms. Pac-Man to give free games. So when Ms. Pac-Man got taken away, Marilla was crowned the All-Time Ms. Pac-Man Champ of Crickenburg because neither me or Dave would ever beat her high score.

So for a while we just complained about the crane game and the stupid toys that were in it. And we made fun of the idiots who spent a dollar to try to grab the stupid toys with the crane.

But then we became those idiots because one day the crane game guy came and put new toys in. It was all the usual stuff—like Care Bears and Simpsons dolls and NASCAR teddy bears—except for one crazy weird item. It was a stuffed-doll version of President Andrew Jackson. We knew it was him because he had a tag that said "Andrew Jackson, Seventh President of the United States of America."

"Why on earth does that exist?" asked Dave.

"And why is it in the crane game?" said Marilla. "I mean, who would want it? I mean, other than us?"

Marilla was right--we did want it. No one knows why, but we wanted it bad.

We each spent a few dollars trying to get it. Finally, Marilla got the crane to come right down on Jackson's head perfectly, but when the crane raised up, he only moved an inch before he slipped off.

"Save your money, kids," said Larry. "He's stuck in there too tight. You'll have to wait for people to get some of that other stuff out of there."

So then we checked the game all the time to see if he'd come loose yet. Our big fear was that someone else would get him first. But he still looked stuck. By the way, Marilla says Andrew Jackson is a different Jackson than the Lee-Jackson Day guy.

Dave suggested we walk down to the Taco Bell for lunch, but Marilla reminded him that her parents said she wasn't allowed to do that anymore.

↑

We easily could have snuck down to Taco Bell and back without Marilla's parents finding out, but Marilla says that since the Ten Commandments say to "honor your mother and father" it's a sin to do something they've told you not to. Meanwhile, Dave is the number-one rule-follower of all time, so if anybody has made a rule—even Marilla's parents—he thinks he has to follow it.

Dave and I decided it wouldn't be fair for us to go without her. So after lunch--we just had more biscuits instead of going to Taco Bell--we adjourned. Marilla had to go watch her little sister so that her mom could take her dad to Roanoke.

↑

He has to go all the time to the dialysis clinic up in Roanoke, which is the closest big city, for his kidneys. I would never say this to Marilla, but he is really, really sick. When I go over to her trailer he hardly even looks up anymore, he just sits at the kitchen table watching Marilla's sister watch The Lion King. I think he needs a kidney transplant really bad.

UNOFFICIAL Personal Note

Marilla's parents don't like for me or Dave to hang around while she's babysitting, so he and I went back to the break room. He was working on a new issue of his comic book, <u>The All-Zombie Marching Band</u>, and I was helping him by typing what the zombies said into the speech balloons.

After Dave went home for supper, I hung around the Qwikpick until my parents' shift ended. The Qwikpick's so close to the trailer park that we just walk back and forth from our house.

On the way home, my dad said somebody had told him that Wal-Mart was going to open a new store.

"You know where they're going to put it, don't you? Right on top of this trailer park! And the town is going to let them do it. Move out those trailers and bring in the money!"

My dad says stuff like this all the time and it never actually happens.

"Maybe they won't build it here," I said. "Maybe they'll build it out of town."

"Oh that's great," he said. "Let's bulldoze some more of the countryside! Let's tear it all down!"

But I actually like to hear my dad going on about stuff like this. It's better than hearing him complain about his job all the time.

ALL-ZOMBIE MARCHING BAND by DAVE

SECTION V
Rhyme-jitsu

Back in school the next week, there were three main things on our minds: the rat and the Spring Concert and Rhyme-jitsu.

What is Rhyme-jitsu?

Rhyme-jitsu is a game that Marilla invented where you have to think of a rhyme that describes what's going on at that exact moment. We were going to call it Rhyme Time but then we watched this hilarious kung fu movie--one of the leftover Qwikpick videos. It's called <u>Ninjitsu Palace of Burning Fist</u> so Marilla decided to call the game Rhyme-jitsu. Now when we say a rhyme, we also say "Hyah!" like a karate man. That makes it a lot more fun, but I do get a little embarrassed about saying "Hyah."

Here's how it works. Like if someone spills their lunch and a cafeteria lady brings out a mop to clean it up, you could say "mop slop" and get a

I'm still waiting for a chance to say "history mystery."

point. You get two points if you can think of a rhyme with two syllables. Like when the cafeteria lady finishes, you could say "stopping mopping." (Nobody had ever gotten a three-syllable one yet. Those are too hard, but we decided you'd get five points for one of those because they are so rare.)

Marilla keeps the score in a special notebook. At that time the score was: Marilla 86, Dave 74, Lyle 80.

Every time that me or Marilla gets one, Dave goes, "I was about to say that."

And every time Dave says that, Marilla says, "You gotta be fast to beat my Burning Fist Rhyme-jitsu."

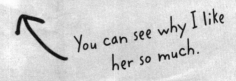

You can see why I like her so much.

All-Time Great
Rhyme-jitsu Rhymes

1. "Best test," by Marilla when she somehow got 103 points on a Civics test.
2. "Spilly chili," by me when Dave spilled his chili at Wendy's.
3. "War bore," by me about this movie we had to watch during World War II week.
4. "Band land," by Marilla. This is what she named the band room at school and now that's what everybody calls it.

I just realized that <u>Qwikpick</u> is a Rhyme-jitsu. Weird.

Extra Rules

1. You can pronounce the words a little funny to make the rhyme work--"awful waffle" rhymes if you say it just right.
2. You can't use a rhyme that's been used before.
3. You can't do something just to make a rhyme out of it. Like petting a cat and saying "pat cat."
4. You can't rhyme using somebody's name--that's too easy. "Dave Gave," "Smile Lyle," "Cruisin' Susan," "Dizzy Lizzie," "Slobby Robbie," et cetera . . .

↑

Don't ever say "Marilla Gorilla" under any circumstances because she'll cream you!

SECTION VI
The Biological Station

At lunch, when everybody else was talking about the Spring Concert or playing paper football or otherwise occupied, Dave passed me and Marilla a piece of paper that he had printed off the Internet. It was the website for the biological station where the Rat with the Human Face was.

The website said that the place is called the Mount Perrin Biological Station and it's run by Murray University, which is the big college way over in Waltonsville. It said people go there to study salamanders, plant diseases, beetle larvae, mice, snails, and all sorts of stuff.

There was a picture of this big building made out of stone.

"That's the laboratory," whispered Dave, "where the rat is."

The strange thing about middle school is that you can try to say something in a normal voice and nobody

pays any attention to you--at least,
they never do to me. But if you whisper
something, it's like you shouted it.

Jeremy Price jumped out of his seat
and grabbed the paper from me.

"What are you guys looking at?" he
said, and then he looked at the paper.
He was probably planning to make fun
of us or tell everybody our secret. But
there wasn't anything there to make fun
of, so he just hocked up a big load of
spit and let it drool out all over the
paper and then handed it back to me.

No one makes me madder than Jeremy
Price--the aforementioned jerk who
threw my calculator on the roof--but
there's little I can do about it. He's
pretty big for someone at the nerd table.

But Marilla is bigger and she jumped
up and grabbed the paper and was about
to smear the spit all over him.

That's when Mrs. Porterfield, our Life
Science teacher, showed up.

"What's going on here, Marilla?" she
asked.

"Jeremy spit all over our stuff," Marilla said.

"Ug, Jeremy, why do you do things like this?"

Jeremy said it was an accident, and it looked like Mrs. Porterfield was going to go. He never seems to get in trouble for anything. He is, in the opinion of the full membership of The Qwikpick Adventure Society, a total jerk who deserves jail time, yet he never even gets sent to the office.

Anyway, there's a point to this whole story, because when Mrs. Porterfield looked at the paper, she said, "Oh! Mount Perrin Biological Station?"

Normally, we would have wanted to keep any information about a Qwikpick Adventure Society trip completely secret, but the paper didn't say anything about the rat or the basement, so we figured it was safe to admit that it was ours.

It was at this moment that we became Mrs. Porterfield's three favorite students.

"Really?" she said. "I never knew you were so interested in biology. Why don't you come back to the science room and look at my Mount Perrin scrapbook? I studied there, you know."

"Really?" said Marilla. "We'd love to learn more about it."

So we all got up to dump our trays and go with her. Mrs. Porterfield handed the spit-covered paper to Jeremy. "Why don't you take this to the principal's office, Jeremy, and explain to him why you spit on it?"

As Marilla pointed out later, this was an incredible double-happiness moment. First, we had found a great source of information about the biological station, and secondly, Jeremy had finally been sent to the office.

Actually, Mrs. Porterfield gave us a lot more information about the biological station than we really needed.

The important thing we found out was that it's only open from May to September.

When she said that, we all looked
at each other and smiled because we
realized that meant we could go up
there and look around without any
problem as long as we went before May.
But just to be sure, Marilla asked, "So
there's nobody up there at all during
the winter?"

"That's right," said Mrs. Porterfield.
"Just the caretaker."

We gave each other another look. It
wasn't going to be so easy after all.

Dave asked, "So who is the caretaker?"
which Marilla later said was a strange
question to ask and could have made
Mrs. Porterfield suspicious.

But she wasn't. She just said, "Oh,
I wouldn't know. It's been years since
I studied up there, you know. That was
when I was getting my college degree.
Those were the happiest summers . . ."

And that was when she started giving
us the parts we didn't need to know,
until the bell rang and we had to go to
Civics class.

"I'll talk to her some more later," said Marilla. "I'll find out what she knows about the basement."

"I don't see what good that'll do," said Dave, "if we don't have any way of getting up there."

"We've got until May," said Marilla. "We've got to figure something out by then."

SECTION VII
Lyle Becomes a Bad Kid

A couple of weeks went by before we figured out how to get to Mount Perrin.

Basically, what happened in those weeks was Dave and Marilla and the rest of the nerd table kept talking about the Spring Concert, Marilla pulled ahead in the Rhyme-jitsu competition, and I got in big trouble for using a bad word.

I would be glad to skip over this, but I need to put it in here because it's all part of how I wound up being labeled a "bad kid" by Marilla's parents. As I've been trying to make clear, I'm not one of the bad kids. Yet the bad kids seem to just keep getting to be bad, while I keep getting hammered.

The first thing I have to tell you about is why I was watching the TV show M*A*S*H. My father decided to cut off our cable TV because it costs so much. He said he was going to put up an antenna but he hasn't done it yet and so I can't get any channels at the trailer.

The TV at the Qwikpick gets one station, though, and that's channel seven. If you can only get one station, channel seven is not the one you would want to get. It mostly shows junk. However, at 5:30 every day it shows M*A*S*H, which is a show about doctors during the Korean War. It's funny even though it's about war. I usually watch it while I eat supper.

Anyway, the star of the show calle d this other guy a "pervert" and it got a big laugh. I wasn't sure exactly what it meant, but I could tell it was a pretty good insult.

So a couple of days later at school, I got to the nerd table before Dave and Marilla, and Jeremy started ragging on me. He doesn't rag on me as much when Marilla is around because he's afraid of her.

But she wasn't there and he started making fun of my glasses again. This drives me crazy because I think they're funny-looking too, but I just keep hoping that people will get used to them. Sadly, that will never happen, because I'm the only person in the world with white glasses. They looked silvery in the glasses store, plus they were big-time on sale.

Jeremy said they make me look like a fashion model. A girl model, of course.

So I said, "Shut up, pervert!"

Jeremy didn't say anything. He just got up and walked to the front of the cafeteria, where the principal was standing. Then he and the principal walked back to the table and the principal told me to please follow him. I couldn't believe it.

He took me to the office and asked me why I had said a bad word.

I said I didn't know it was a bad word.

He got out his dictionary, looked up <u>pervert</u>, and read: "One who has turned away from what is good or morally right. One who favors abnormal . . . er . . . Well, I better not say that word at all. Bad stuff."

That sounded pretty bad and I started to think I really had done something bad, and so I didn't even really try to defend myself against the principal.

"Does that seem like a nice thing to say about someone?" he asked.

I had to admit no.

"Then why would you say that about another student? You claim you didn't know it was bad. Did you think it was good?"

I had to admit no.

"Then you must have known it was bad," he said. "Why do you feel the need to call people bad names?"

It went on like this for a long time. When he finally let me go, all I had time to do was go back to lunch and dump my tray before Civics class. I didn't want to tell Marilla about it because she doesn't like people who cuss. But I asked Dave about it later and he said he didn't think it was a bad word at all. Had I just gotten in trouble for saying a word that wasn't really bad?

That night I asked Larry about it. Larry is someone you can ask about stuff like this.

He said he couldn't believe I got sent to the office for saying "pervert." He said it was basically like calling someone a creep or a weirdo. He said he'd call up my principal for me and teach him some real bad words.

I told him not to do that, but what he said made me feel better. It also made me mad too, because kids at school, even Jeremy, use real cuss words all the time and never get in trouble. And I say one word that isn't even a cuss word and I have to go to the office and I wind up being a "bad kid." And I'm sure they're all thinking "those trailer park kids sure pick up some bad words," which is extra dumb because I learned the word from a show about doctors!

SECTION VIII
Marilla's Plan and
Dave's Money

Anyway, that's the biggest thing that happened while we were trying to figure out how to get up to the rat's basement.

About a week later, Marilla found the answer, though she didn't think she had at first.

"I almost had a way for us to get up to Mount Perrin," she told us at lunch. "But it turned out to cost too much."

"How much?" I asked.

"Forty dollars! Each!" she said. "It was a rec center trip. You know how my dad goes down to the rec center for aqua therapy? Well, last night I went with him, and while I was waiting around I was looking at the bulletin board and saw a sign about the trip. It goes up to the Mount Perrin Hotel for Easter brunch."

"Yeah, they've got a huge buffet up there," said Dave. "They've got these big ice sculptures and shrimp and crab legs. I bet it's even bigger for Easter."

"Well, I guess that's why it costs so much," said Marilla. "But that stinks, because we don't want all that junk."

"Maybe we could see if we could pay for just the van ride and not the brunch?" I suggested.

"Maybe," said Marilla doubtfully.

"Let's go down there after school and ask," said Dave.

So we did.

The rec center is only a little ways down South Franklin Street from the Qwikpick, but of course you can't walk down South Franklin Street anymore because of the bypasses, the on-ramps, and the crazy Wal-Mart traffic. But the road that runs through the trailer park goes almost all the way down there. Then you can cut through the parking lot of this weird place

called Lyndo-Tech that makes spark
plugs or something. Then you just run
across Depot Street to the rec center.

You might think it would be really
great to live near the rec center, but
unless you want to join a basketball
league there's nothing to do there.
Why would I want to join a basketball
league? Playing basketball in school
is the most miserable thing in the
universe.

One time I looked through the door
into the gymnasium when the basketball
league was playing. Most of the kids
were the same jerks from my PE class.
The big difference was that in PE they
act like they know everything in the
world about bask etball. But at the rec
center all their dads were there, and
their dads were yelling "Move the ball"
and "Don't let him do that" and "Push
the D" and other stuff that made it
seem like they didn't know anything. I
almost felt sorry for them but I didn't,
bec ause they all yell the same stuff

at me on the very rare occasions when
I actually touch the ball in PE.

Anyway, we got to the rec center and
asked who was in charge of the trips
and they told us to go to the Senior
Room and ask for Terri.

So we walked past the gym and
weight rooms and stuff. We looked in
one of the gyms and sure enough there
was a basketball league playing.

"Same lame game," I said, but
I didn't get any points because I
already got points for it when I said
it the first time in PE. (You get an
extra point if you can make three
words rhyme.)

Then we started to hear this
wild noise. We followed the signs to
the Senior Room and the noise kept
getting louder. It was like hyenas or
something.

We got to the room and there were
about ten old ladies sitting around
a huge table with a quilt on it. They
were all sewing on the quilt and

laughing and shouting. I think they may have been telling dirty jokes.

"Built quilt?" said Dave.

"That rhymes, but it doesn't make sense," said Marilla.

They stopped laughing when they saw us, and started saying "Come on in, sugar" and "Who you looking for, sweetie?"

We said we were looking for Terri, and this incredibly tan woman came bouncing out of a little room.

She was very friendly but very surprised to find out we wanted to go on a trip. It turned out that the trips are basically for the old ladies. But Terri said we could go if we wanted to as long as our parents signed a release form.

"Like a permission slip from school? That's a trip slip," I said. "Hyah!"

"Well, it's actually several pages long," said Terri. She looked like she thought I was weird. I guess she wasn't used to dealing with kids, just old people.

Marilla hadn't even noticed my Rhyme-jitsu. As she said later, she was busy thinking about the permission slip and how tough that was going to be since her parents didn't even want her to go to Taco Bell.

Then Dave asked about the price and if we could just pay for the van ride and not the brunch.

Terri didn't like that. Not one bit. She was still friendly, but she sort of made us feel dumb for asking.

"If you don't want the brunch, then you shouldn't go on the trip."

That's when Dave said, "That's okay. We'll pay the full price."

"Okay," said Terri, "I'll need a ten-dollar deposit from each of you."

"Uh, we need to talk about that for a second," I said.

The full price? Forty bucks? He had to be insane.

I didn't have forty dollars and I didn't have ten dollars either.

"Okay," she said, "but I can't put you on the list until you pay the deposit. But I'll go ahead and get those forms for your parents to sign."

As soon as she turned around, Marilla and I were both about to tell Dave it was too much money, but he knew what we were going to say, and said, "Guys, just let me loan you the money for now. This is our only chance to get up there."

UNOFFICIAL Personal Note

Dave can really drive me crazy sometimes! Where was I going to get forty dollars to pay him back? Forty dollars to him is not the same as forty dollars to me. Marilla was probably thinking the same thing, but before we could get out of it Terri came back and Dave got out his Velcro wallet and handed her thirty dollars for our deposits. What was he doing with thirty dollars anyway?

It all happened so fast! Dave
paying and Terri taking the money.
As soon as we got out of the room,
Marilla asked Dave to go back.

"Let's just ask for the deposit back.
That's too much money. And I'm not
sure I can get my parents to sign the
slip."

"Yeah, Dave," I said, "I can't spend
forty bucks. I'd rather not go."

"You don't want to go?"

"Not for forty bucks," I said.

"Well, don't worry about it, then.
You don't have to pay me back. It's a
present."

Neither of us said thank you right
then. I felt really, really weird
about it, but I didn't know what to
say.

"What's the big deal?" said Dave.
"It's my grandma's money. She's always
giving me and my brothers money. I'll
be getting more at Passover."

UNOFFICIAL Personal Note

But it <u>was</u> a big deal. For a lot of reasons, including this one: It seemed like another place where Dave is winning in regard to Marilla. They're in band together, she has his origami Pegasus in her locker, and now he's treating her to a fancy trip. If I didn't go along, it would be like a date almost.

SECTION IX
Convincing Our Parents

Obviously, we weren't going to tell
our parents about the Rat with the
Human Face--that would have ruined
everything. But we were going to have
to tell them something to get the
permission slips signed.

I had it the easiest. I told my
parents that Dave had invited me to
go as his guest, which was basically
the truth since he was paying. I
didn't tell them how much it cost
because they wouldn't have liked
that. Since they were both working
Easter Day, Mom said she was glad I'd
have something to do other than hang
around the Qwikpick. Me too! I mean,
I love the Qwikpick, but it does get
boring sometimes when I'm by myself.

Dave told his parents about the
trip, but didn't tell them that he was
paying for me and Marilla. His family
was getting together for Passover,
so his co usins would be in town. His

mother thought he should stick around
the house and play with his cousins,
but he pointed out that the last time
his cousins came over, they, along with
his dumb twin brothers, started doing
pro wrestling moves on the trampoline
and then one of them grabbed him and
body slammed him and he hurt his neck
and everyone got in trouble. So his
mother agreed to let him go, but she
reminded him that since it was still
Passover he couldn't pig out at the
buffet and could only eat eggs mostly.
That didn't matter, though, since
we weren't actually going to eat the
buffet.

   But Marilla really had a hard time.
Her family doesn't celebrate Easter,
so that wasn't a problem, but her mom
said it sounded a lot like a date and
that she was way too young to go on a
date. Marilla said it absolutely was
not a date but more like a field trip
and she explained how Terri was going
to be there and everything. But her
mother still said no.

I wasn't there to see it, but from
what Marilla told me there was a
really huge fight between her and
her mom. Then finally her dad, who I
don't th ink has the energy left for a
fight, said, "Oh, just let her go. She's
cooped up in this trailer too much."

Nobody ever argues with her dad
anymore so she got to go.

UNOFFICIAL Personal Note

This time I can skip a few weeks ahead, since nothing worth putting in the official report happened. At school, it was basically just a lot more about the Spring Concert.

The worst thing was that the band started practicing for the Spring Concert every day after school. So that meant I was stuck at the Qwikpick every day without Marilla and Dave. It was too cold to do anything outside. Larry saw that I was bored out of my gourd and tried to teach me how to juggle. I actually started to get pretty good because there was absolutely nothing to do but practice. I got Dad to time it for me and I can actually juggle for ten seconds. That may not sound like much but it is a lot, believe me.

I also read a bunch of books. The best one was this great book by Lloyd Alexander called <u>The Book of Three</u>.

It's the first book in a series and it's absolutely incredible. But the library doesn't have the second book. They have the first book and the fifth book, but not the books in between. What is the point of that? Who's ever going to read the fifth book if they can't read the middle books?

SECTION X
The Planning Session

We got together at the Qwikpick on
the Thursday before Easter. We had
that Friday off from school but Dave
and Marilla were going to be busy, so
Thursday was our best time to have a
planning session since there was no
band practice for once.

We said hi to my parents, who were
working downstairs, and checked on
Andrew Jackson. Dave thought maybe
it was loose now, so he played once
and couldn't get it to budge. Then he
fussed about what a rip-off it was. By
the way, Marilla wrote a poem about
the crane game one time. Here it is:

Once Andrew Jackson
was trapped behind glass.

The crane couldn't get him
because it moved too fast.

We put in our buck,

But never had luck.

The crane game sure is a pain
in the . . . posterior!

Larry told us again not to waste our money on the crane game. Then he gave us a bag of weird potato chips. It was a new flavor--eggplant ranch--and he wanted to know if they were any good. We told him they were the best things we had ever tasted--which they were!--and he gave us the rest of the bag. Then we got some drinks and went upstairs to the break room.

Dave got out a map that he had downloaded from the Internet. It was a government topo map, he said, that mostly showed where the mountains went up and down, but it also had the hotel and the biological station on it.

At first it just looked like a lot of lines, but it was really easy to see where the Mount Perrin Hotel was because it's on a big lake and the lake was the only big blue blob on the map. Dave said the hotel was at one end of the lake and the biological station was at the other.

"The lake is a mile long," he said. "We can either go down the road or take the nature trail that goes around the lake. I think that would be faster.

"Either way, a mile will probably take us about twenty minutes. We can look for the rat for fifty minutes, then head back--that's another twenty minutes--and the whole thing will take an hour and a half.

"I'm sure it will take the other people at least that long to eat. The restaurant at the hotel is really fancy and I bet those old ladies sit there for hours. We may even get back in time to grab some food."

UNOFFICIAL Personal Note

It's a little frustrating the way Dave planned the whole trip out like he was the leader. I wouldn't mind if Marilla was the leader, but I don't want Dave to boss me around. It's not that I don't like Dave—he's my best friend after all—I just don't like getting shown up in front of Marilla. But he does have good ideas sometimes. Still, the planning session was basically just Dave telling us what to do.

Marilla said she would bring her camera along so that we could hopefully bring back a picture of the rat.

"I'll bring my first-aid kit," said Dave. "In case someone gets bitten by the rat."

This was the first time I had thought of the possibility of getting bitten by the rat.

"Do you think the rat bites?" I asked.

"Of course it bites! How do you think it eats?" said Dave. "Plus, actually, I heard a story about this guy who fell asleep in a cave and he had a dream that naked ladies were kissing him and when he woke up it turned out to be rats eating his face."

"Dis-gust," said Marilla.

"The important thing is to never get the rat into a corner," said Dave. "That makes them panic and then they go crazy."

Dave had never seen a rat in his life, of course—this is all just stuff he heard at camp probably.

"One thing's been worrying me," said Marilla. "This caretaker guy. When we went to the poop plant we thought no one would be there because it was Christmas. And we were wrong and almost got busted. What if we go to all this trouble to go up there and we run right into the caretaker?"

Dave didn't have an answer for that.

The last order of business was a special announcement that Marilla made.

"You know how we're practically tied at Rhyme-jitsu?" she said. "Well, why don't we make Sunday the championship day. Whoever has the high score at the end of the day wins."

"What do they win?" I asked.

"Glory," said Marilla. "The winner will be the Rhyme-jitsu Master of All Time!"

Marilla showed us the score book. The score was Marilla 126, Lyle (me) 116, Dave 124.

"That's not fair," I said. "I'm ten points behind. I'll never catch up."

"Well, it's got to end sooner or later," said Marilla. "Besides, I've always warned you that your Crab Style is no match for my Burning Fist rhymes."

Well, I figured I wouldn't mind too much if Marilla won, but if Dave did I'd be mad!

SECTION XI
The Bus Ride

Easter morning we met at the Qwikpick.

The first thing you see when you walk in the door is the crane game. So we saw right away that Andrew Jackson was gone!

"I can't believe it!" said Dave.

"Who could have gotten it? Nobody could have wanted it as much as us," said Marilla.

"I bet someone was trying to get a lousy Care Bear and they got Andrew Jackson by accident," Lyle (me) said. "They probably don't even understand why it's such a jacked-up thing to own."

We should have realized that Andrew Jackson's disappearance was more than just a bummer, it was an omen--a sign telling us that today was going to be a bigger disaster than falling into a poop fountain.

But like I said, we didn't know

that, so we walked on down to the rec center.

We got there at 10:45, fifteen minutes early, but everybody else was already there. And everybody else was an old lady. It was all the ladies we had seen working on the quilt plus some more. I couldn't believe how loud they were.

Once we got on the bus--actually, one of those things that is like a van with half a bus stuck on the back--they seem ed even louder. They were nice to us, but we felt totally like outsiders because we weren't old people. But that was okay, we just needed a ride.

One woman started talking about two certain parts of her body. I'm not going to say what she called them, but if you said it at school you'd get in huge trouble. It was a lot worse than pervert, I know that. The woman next to her said, "Hush, Millie, the kids are listening."

My ears turned red, which they do sometimes,
and it's extra embarrassing because they stick out
so much. The ladies laughed even harder.

"It's nothing they haven't heard
before, is it, kids?"

We were way too embarrassed to say
anything.

Terri started driving the bus
and the first few minutes were just
driving past the Qwikpick and the
Wal-Mart and all the usual stuff. But
after about twenty minutes we were
passing Waltonsville, which is where
the big college is. I had only seen
that a few times, and once we passed
that we were in places I had never
seen.

The ladies kept talking like crazy.
I guess they had seen all this before.

We each got a few Rhyme-jitsus in
about stuff we saw out the window.
The best one was probably Marilla's
"horse source" when we saw a big
stable on a horse farm, but Dave got
two points for "we see tree," which was
so dumb it shouldn't have counted.

I got some too but I couldn't seem
to catch up. It looked like the real
compe tition was between Marilla and
Dave, who were practically tied now.

We went up a steep little
mountain--I was afraid the bus was
going to start rolling backward--and
then right back down the other side.
Then we turned off the highway onto a
regular road.

"Just Seven Miles to Mount Perrin
Hotel, Home of Virginia's Scecnic
Wonder, Mount Perrin Lake!" said a
big sign.

"Did you see that?" said Marilla.
"They spelled 'scenic' wrong."

"Maybe the lake is so good that it's
not just scenic, it's also skeknik,"
said Dave.

"Hotel no spell," I said. "Hyah! Two
more points. I'm catching up!"

"Hmmm," said Dave, "I guess that
counts."

"Just barely," said Marilla.

I had been a little disappointed

that the hotel was only seven miles
away. That didn't sound like much
of a trip. But then we started going
up and up and up and the bus went
slower and slower. We would go around
these turns and you could look down
over the edge and see way, way down.
I was a little scar ed and a little
carsick. Terri seemed like a good
driver, though. I guess that's an
important part of her job.

We passed a little cluster of
trailers. It would be really cool to
live way out there on the mountain.
As long as Marilla and Dave lived out
there too.

After a while we didn't pass any
more houses. Just trees and more
trees. Then we saw some little patches
of snow under some trees.

"Did you guys see that snow?" I
asked. "It hasn't snowed in weeks."

"It has up here," said an old lady.
I didn't even know she was listening.
"It's a lot colder up on the moun
tain, so when we get rain sometimes

they get snow. Also, the snow takes a lot longer to melt because of the low temperatures."

I got the feeling that this old lady must have been a teacher. She seemed like she knew what she was talking about. And she was pretty nice.

"How much colder is it?" Marilla asked her.

"Usually about fifteen degrees less. It was probably about fifty this morning in Crickenburg, so it'll be thirty-five or so up here."

"Snow no go--hyah!" said Dave all of a sudden, which made the woman look at him funny then turn around and start talking to someone else.

None of us had coats on, just jackets. I was glad my mom had made me wear a sweater, since she said the hotel dining room was probably kind of fancy. Dave's mom had made him wear a tie, which he had taken off before we even got on the bus. Marilla said her mom had tried to get her to wear a skirt, which would have been way too cold. We

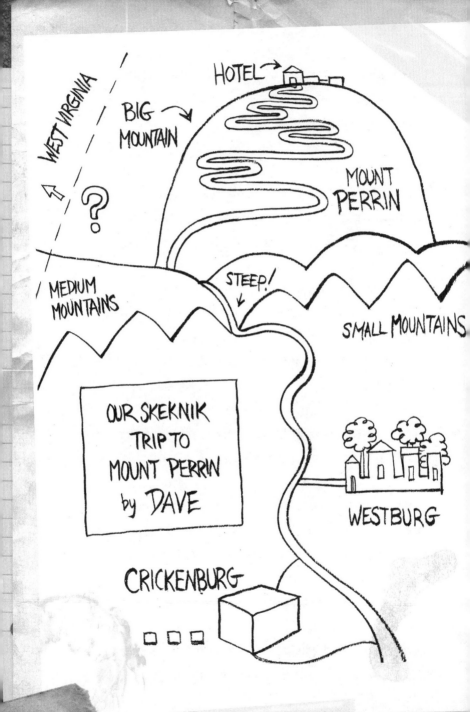

were going to have to walk a long way, after all.

"Here it comes, kids," the teacher-type lady said to us.

The bus popped over a hump all of a sudden and leveled out and there in front of us was a huge lake, right on top of the mountain. And next to us was about the biggest building I've ever seen. It was the hotel, made totally out of stone. There were all these little log cabins around it too.

"Very skeknik," said Marilla.

We got out of the bus and it was freezing! It was colder than it had been at Christmas, when we went to the poop fountain.

"Oh my God, guys, we are going to freeze," I said.

"Don't say 'God,' Lyle," said Marilla. "But you're right, it is freezing."

"Sorry, guys, I didn't expect this," said Dave. "I've only been up here in the summer and it's nice and cool then."

"It's nice and cool now too," said Marilla.

Next came a big moment that we had talked about a lot. Obviously, we were going to have to get away from Terri and the old ladies. We had rehearsed exactly what to say so that neither Marilla the saint or Dave the number-one rule-follower of all time would have to lie.

Basically, I was going to be the one stretching the truth as far as I could.

I'm not a saint and not even the number-two rule-follower of all time, but I didn't want to have to lie either.

"Terri, is it okay if we go down to the lake?"

"Sure," she said, looking at her watch. "Be back soon, though. It's twelve-fifteen right now and we eat at twelve-thirty."

"Well," I said, "we're not really hungry. We were kind of hoping to look around more."

Terri didn't seem to like this.

"You're not going to eat?" she said. "But you paid for it."

Dave and Marilla didn't say anything, so I had to keep talking.

"I've never seen the lake before and there's supposed to be a really cool path that goes around it and . . ."

"All right," she said, "but you paid for it. You should at least come back in time to get something to eat."

UNOFFICIAL Personal Note

I've noticed that adults get completely hung up on whether something has been paid for. I mean, I hate to waste money, but if I don't want something why should I be forced to eat it? When my grandma was still alive she would eat all kinds of old, gross food. Even stuff with mold on it. She would just cut off the mold and eat it. "This cost three ninety-nine a pound," she would say. "I'm not going to throw it away."

Anyway, Terri finally let us go
and Dave led us through the hotel
lobby, which was really awesome and
had a big stuffed bear in it. I mean
a real dead stuffed bear. And a Civil
War cannon. Not the wheels, just
the barrel part on a board over the
fireplace.

Dave asked at the counter for a
trail map. I hate to ask for stuff
from adults at places like this--not
that I've been any other places
exactly like this--but Dave never
seems to mind.

"Why do we need a map?" Marilla
asked. "I thought you said the trail
goes around the lake."

"It never hurts to have a map," said
Dave, who already had several other
maps in his pocket. "Let's go."

SECTION XII
Around the Lake

We went out of the lobby and onto this giant stone porch that looked over the lake.

"Let me get a picture," said Marilla. She took a couple pictures of the lake. Then this guy came over and said he'd take a picture of all three of us standing at the railing with the lake behind us.

"Do you work here?" asked Dave.

"Yep," the guy said. He looked like maybe he was a high school student.

"What do you do?" Marilla asked.

"I pick up cigarette butts," he said.

"Really?" I asked.

"Yeah, can you believe it?"

I saw that he had a little bucket full of cigarette butts, so I believed it.

"Hey," said Dave, "how long would it take us to walk down to the other end of the lake?"

"You mean on the trail? About twenty minutes, I guess."

Dave seemed very pleased that he had planned correctly.

"But," the guy said, "the trail is closed."

"What?" said Dave. "Why?"

"I don't know. They just close the trails all winter."

Marilla started to say that it wasn't winter anymore, but Dave said, "C'mon, we'll have to hurry if we're going to take the road."

"Oh, yeah," the guy said, "that's going to take you like forty minutes, because it winds around a lot."

"Oh crap," said Dave. "We better get going."

We thanked the guy and took off. Dave was walking like crazy and trying to read his maps at the same time.

"We're not going to have enough time," he said. "Forty minutes there and forty minutes back and that's almost our whole hour and a half. We'll have to run."

So we did. At least it warmed us up some. But after about five minutes of running, we couldn't run anymore.

"I've got to stop," I said. "I've got like a cramp or something in my side."

"Keep going," said Dave, who was already getting ahead of us. "This cost a hundred and twenty bucks. We've got to make the most of it!"

"I've got to stop," I said again, and I did.

Marilla hadn't said anything since we started running--I think she was out of breath--but now she wheezed, "Cash dash. Hyah." It was a pretty weak <u>hyah</u> for her, but it put her back in the lead.

"At least keep walking," said Dave. "C'mon."

Dave kept going and got way ahead of us.

When we finally got to the end of the road, he had been waiting there for a while.

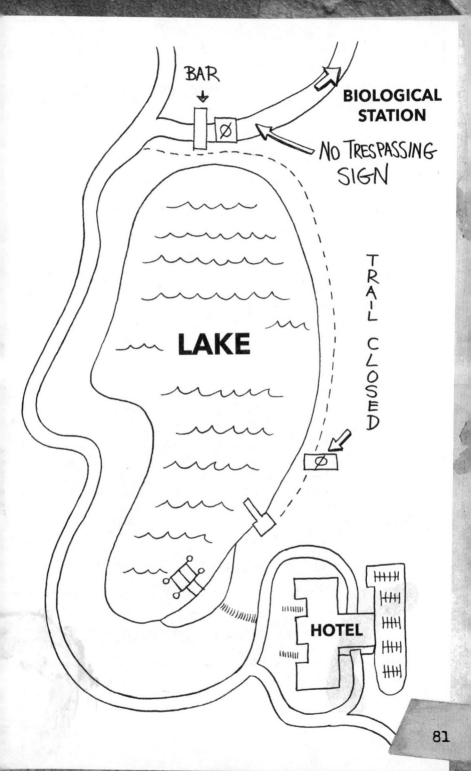

"Guys, we have a problem," he said. "Look!"

Where the road ended, there was another gravel road that went off into the woods. There was a big wooden sign that said "Mount Perrin Biological Station." There was a metal bar that went across the road and there was a sign on it that said "Private Property."

"That gate is locked and the sign says no trespassing," said Dave.

"I know, I can read," said Marilla.

"Well, I guess we shouldn't do it, then," said Dave, who as I've said is the number-one rule-follower of all time.

"Yeah . . . maybe not," said Marilla, who did not want to commit a sin.

"You're not going to turn around now, are you?" I asked.

"Well, what can we do?" asked Dave. "I don't want to get in trouble."

"But you knew we were going to be going somewhere we weren't supposed to go, didn't you?" I asked.

"I didn't know there was going to be a sign telling me not to," said Dave. "There wasn't a sign like that at the poop plant."

"What about the hundred and twenty bucks?" I asked.

So we all ducked under the gate and kept walking, even though none of us wanted to.

UNOFFICIAL Personal Note

Dave looked like he was about to cry. Even for him, $120 is a lot of money to throw away because you saw a sign. I wasn't trying to be mean, it just seemed like a natural question to ask. But I guess maybe it's evidence that I really am a bad kid, because both of them agreed to go after I said that. But if it wasn't for the $120, I would have turned back too. I just didn't want to waste Dave's money.

SECTION XIII
The Laboratory

"I just thought of something," I said. "If that gate was locked, maybe the caretaker keeps the laboratory locked too. We might not even be able to get in."

Nobody said anything. We really weren't having much fun right at that moment.

It seemed like we were walking into the middle of the wilderness, nothing but trees all around us. But then we went around a curve and there was another big building that looked a lot like the hotel. It was made out of the same color stones and was also huge.

"Duh," I almost said, but I didn't because that's not a very nice thing to say to your friend, especially when he's already miserable and sorry he came. So instead I said, "Good job, Dave," to try to get him back in the spirit of the adventure.

There was a sign that said "Lab Parking" that pointed to an empty parking lot.

"This must be it," said Dave, looking at his map.

There was nobody around, but there was a broken-down pickup truck near the lab building.

There was a door on the side of the stone building. We went up and peeked through the glass. It was dark inside.

"It looks safe," I whispered, and reached for the handle. It was locked.

"Oh no," whispered Dave. "Lyle was right. The whole place is locked up. This is a disaster!"

"Maybe there's another door," whispered Marilla.

We tried to go quietly and sneakily. We peeked around the corner of the

building. Nobody was there, so we went
around to the front. From there we
could see a bunch of other buildings
that I guess are where the scientists
live in the summer.

It felt like any second the
caretaker was going to come out of one
of the buildings and catch us. When
we got to the front steps, I ran up,
tried the door, and ran back down.

"Locked."

We went around to the back of
the building and that's when we
discovered the strangest thing. The
steps to the basement were on the
outside of the building. They just
went right down into the ground and
there was a door at the bottom that
went right under the laboratory. The
door had one of those metal latches
that you can put a lock on, but there
wasn't a lock.

The basement was open! In five
seconds we were down the stairs and
going through the door.

SECTION XIV
The Basement, A.K.A.
the Lair of the Rat
with the Human Face

The electrician was right. It smelled really weird.

We stepped inside. Unfortunately, the door had a spring on it that made it close automatically. When it closed behind us, things were really, really dark. Dave opened the door again and said, "I'll hold it open. Look for a light switch."

There was enough light coming through that we could see some of the stuff near us. We were in a short hallway that was piled with all sorts of science junk. There were butterfly nets that were nasty and dirty and had gross stuff stuck in them. I think the scientists were using them to catch something a lot slimier than butterflies. There were boxes with all kinds of junk in them, a big old machine that didn't look like it did anything, and lots of PVC pipe and empty flowerpots.

We saw the switch right next to a big dark doorway that led into total darkness.

Marilla flipped the switch but it didn't do anything.

"I guess it doesn't work," she said. "I guess that electrician didn't really fix it."

"Great," Dave muttered. "How are we going to see the rat in the dark?"

I had almost forgotten about the rat. Somehow I had a picture of seeing the rat in broad daylight from a distance. Like when you see a squirrel run up a tree. Seeing a mutant rat in a dark narrow hallway didn't sound so great.

That's when I heard a noise from the other end of the hall. It must have come from around the corner. Kind of a dragging sound.

"Did you hear that?" asked Marilla.

Then it came again. Getting louder every time. Getting closer.

"That can't be a rat," whispered Marilla.

Then there was a loud crash.

"*&$%@," said a voice. Of course, what it actu ally said was a bad word. A <u>really</u> bad word. So I'm just going to use the special typewriter keys like in the comics. Even Larry doesn't talk that bad.

"The caretaker!" whispered Marilla. I know it's weird for me to put an exclamation point on a whisper, but that's how it was.

There were two things we could do at that point. We could run out the door or we could go through the dark doorway that was right there and try to hide.

We didn't have time to vote on it or discuss it or anything. We had to make an instant decision and we all decided the same way at the same time. It felt like running would have meant giving up on the rat, so without saying anything we all went through the doorway into the next room. Since Dave wasn't holding the door open anymore, it closed--pretty quietly, thank goodness--and the basement became one hundred percent dark.

We couldn't see anything, but we could hear the caretaker getting closer and closer.

"@#$&@% lights! How am I supposed to haul this $%#& through the %$#@& dark? $@$%@& electrician!" And on and on. It was basically nonstop bad words. I wish I could talk to Jeremy like that.

It took forever for the caretaker to get down the hallway. It sounded like he was bumping into stuff the whole way. We just stood there in the dark. We had no idea what was in the room with us. I was afraid that if I moved I would bump into something too and it would all be over. If he hadn't been cussing so much, I'm sure he would have heard us breathing.

Then there was light again because he had opened the basement door. We could see the caretaker now. He was carrying something huge and probably heavy. If

he had looked into our room, he would
have seen us, but he didn't.

"$&#@$% door," he said, and then he
was gone and then it got dark again.

"That was--," started Dave, but then
we heard a sound. It was the sound of
metal against metal. <u>Clack, clack</u>, and
then a loud click.

Then we heard more thumping and
cussing as the caretaker dragged
whatever it was up the stairs.

"I think he just locked the door,"
said Marilla. And she was right.

We gave the caretaker a few minutes
to drag his stuff away, then we slowly
went back into the hall and I felt
around for the door handle.

"Yep, it's locked," I said.

"Are you pulling on it?" asked Dave.

"I'm pushing and pulling," I said.
"It moves about a millimeter. It's
definitely locked."

"Let me try," he said. That didn't work
either.

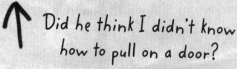 Did he think I didn't know
how to pull on a door?

Dave's mother is a real estate agent and he always thinks he knows everything about houses and stuff.

"Maybe there's another door," I said.

"Doubt it," said Dave. "You never see basements with two doors."

"And how could we find it anyway?" asked Marilla. "It's totally dark and we've got to get out of here fast! What time is it?"

Suddenly, there was a little blue light.

"Look," said Dave. "My watch lights up. We can use it to see where we're going."

It did actually work a little bit. You could just barely see what was right in front of his watch. It made ever ything look blue and spooky. Then the blue light went out.

"It only stays on for five seconds," said Dave, and he pushed the button again and the light turned back on.

"Oh yeah," said Dave. "It's twelve-fifty-six. We've got one hour and four minutes to get back."

I felt like my stomach died. How were we going to get out of there?

"We'll have to bang on the door and get the caretaker to let us out," I said.

"Wait!" said Dave. "That's a worst-case scenario."

"Actually, I think the worst-case scenario is that we bang on the door and the caretaker doesn't let us out," said Marilla.

"And we die and the Rat with the Human Face eats us," I added.

"Just hold on," said Dave. "I mean we should wait before we give up and bang on the door. Maybe Lyle's right and there's another door. Or maybe the caretaker will come back for more stuff and we can sneak out. Who knows? I think we should try every option first before we give up and let the caretaker know we're here. We need to try to

get out of this without any adult
entanglements."

"True," said Marilla, and I had
to agree too. I didn't want to get
yelled at by the caretaker. Of course,
compared to what actually happened,
just getting yelled at by the
caretaker would have been getting off
easy.

SECTION XV
Exploring by Flashlight

"Man, I should have brought a flashlight," said Dave. "That's a must-have item for any hike that involves--"

"Marilla's camera!" I interrupted. As soon as Dave had said the word <u>flash</u>, it reminded me of the camera. "We can use the flash to see where we're going."

"Great idea," said Marilla, "but the batteries won't last forever. Let me turn the camera on. It takes a minute to start up."

We heard the camera beep. Then we stood there in the dark and waited.

"I wonder if the rat can see us in the dark," I said. And even as I said it, this creepy sensation went all over my face and down my back. "I mean, it must be in here somewhere with us right now!"

It seemed like Marilla's camera was taking forever.

"It's on," she said finally. "Now I have to wait for the flash to charge."

There was a little noise somewhere among the boxes of junk. It was exactly the kind of sound a rat would make.

"Why don't you go ahead and take a picture as soon as it's ready," said Dave, "just in case there's something nearby."

"Okay," said Marilla, and suddenly the flash went off and we had this image of a supernova burned permanently onto our eyeballs. We had gotten so used to the dark that it was like the room had exploded.

"I can't see anything at all now," I said.

"Bright light. Hyah!" said Dave. "Lame, but I'll take my point anyway. That makes it Marilla 142, Dave 140." My score was now 130, not that it mattered.

"I've got an idea," said Marilla. "Next time, we'll close our eyes before I hit the flash, then we'll look at the picture on the camera's little screen. Here, I'll load up the picture I just took."

She did, and once our eyes recovered
from the flash, we looked at the
screen and finally saw where we were
standing.

The same hallway full of junk. No
sign of the rat, but we could see more
of the junk and we could see there
were a bunch more doors.

We decided to go into each room and
let Marilla use her camera flash, just
in case we could see a way out.

First we went back to the dark room
we had hidden in.

"Okay, shut your eyes," said Marilla.

Even with our eyes shut the flash
still seemed like a fireball, but it
wasn't nearly as bad. Then we looked at
Marilla's camera to see the picture.

The walls all the way around the
room were lined with shelves and
the shelves were packed with jars.
Hundreds and hundreds of glass jars.
They looked like they were full of
something, but you couldn't see what.

"No door in here," said Dave.

I knew we were in trouble and I knew we were in a hurry, but I also knew I'd always wonder what was in those jars.

"Hold on," I said. "Remember the electrician said there were jars with weird stuff in them? Maybe these are the ones. Marilla, can you take a close-up of what's in the jars?"

"I'll try. Let me change the camera setting." I heard her feet shuffle over to the shelves. "Okay, I'm right next to the jars. Close your eyes."

When we looked at the camera screen I couldn't believe what I saw.

"Oh my God," I said, and Marilla didn't tell me not to say it.

Inside a jar was some kind of insane monster swamp mummy, disgusting in every possible way, and it was so big it was folded in half just to fit in the jar!

Now I realize it must have been a salamander or something, but I never knew that salamanders got that big. This thing was huge and it was a gross gray color like it had been a real color once but had lost it.

We were in a room with hundreds of jars like it, all holding hideous, super-freaky creatures. I was ready to run.

"I gotta do another one," said Marilla. "Close your eyes."

This picture showed two upside-down ghost frogs. The next picture showed three jars all crammed with small salamanders. And the one after that had an enormous rotting snake that must have been ten feet long if you pulled it out of the jar and straightened it out.

"These pictures are totally awesome," said Marilla. "I could sell these."

I can't imagine who would want to buy photos of dead salamanders, except maybe for an album cover for a weird rock band.

"All right, guys, we gotta get moving," said Dave, and he turned on his watch to help us find the door.

Compared to the jar room the rest of the bas ement was pretty boring. Some rooms smelled worse than others, but none had anything but piles of junk and moldy cardboard boxes. ("Old mold," I said, for one point.)

At the end of the hall, there was a turn and then another hall. Marilla took a picture and we saw that this hall was really short and only had one door. We went in and she took another picture. Inside this room were hundreds of little round dishes like we had used once in Mrs. Porterfield's Life Science class to study pond scum. There were also all kinds of glass bottles in weird shapes with weird nozzles and stuff coming off them.

But no door. No windows. No way out.

"All right," said Dave, "it's one-seventeen now. I say we wait until one-thirty and see if he comes back.

If not, we start banging on the door. Then we'll have thirty minutes to get back to the hotel."

"Let's wait in here," I said. "It's nice having a room without dead animals in it."

"No," said Dave, "we need to go back to the jar room so we can slip out the door if he comes back."

We went back to the jar room and sat down against the wall so that the caretaker wouldn't see us even if he looked in the room.

Like I said, it's frustrating when Dave acts like the boss, but he is good at it. This did seem like a good idea.

UNOFFICIAL Personal Note

We sat there for about a minute,
then something touched my hand. At
first I jumped but then I realized it was
Marilla. She squeezed my hand a little
bit and then we just sat there holding
hands. Her hands were so smooth. My
stomach felt weird again but not like it
was dead anymore.

Except for the fact that I was
trapped in a basement with a Rat with
a Human Face, you'd think this would
have been the happiest time of my whole
life because I was holding hands with
Marilla. But I was too busy thinking
about something. See, Marilla was
sitting between me and Dave and I
didn't know if she was holding his hand
too. You can see that it would make a big
difference. If she was holding both our
hands, then she was just being nice and
holding them in a friendly way. But if

she was only holding my hand and not
his, then it meant something else. And
whatever it meant I meant it back,
but I didn't know if it meant that.
I wished I could have seen her other
hand!

SECTION XVI
Up Close and Personal with the Rat with the Human Face

Then came a noise, and not from one of us.

"The caretaker! Shhh," whispered Dave. Marilla let go of my hand. I got up into a crouching position, ready to spring for the door as soon as we got a chance. I couldn't wait to get out of there. What a relief . . .

But no, it wasn't him. The noise wasn't coming from outside. It was inside. Maybe in the hall. Just a little scuffle sound.

Dave turned on his watch. I thought I saw a shape in the doorway. Like a small cat or, actually, like a large rat.

"Something's in the hall," I whispered.

"The rat," said Marilla, and she fired off her camera with no warning. We were blinded again. It took a minute before I could see the picture

that came up on her camera. There was
the doorway and there was like a blurry
lump that might have been the rear
end of a rat. But because she couldn't
see what she was doing, Marilla had
aimed the camera wrong and missed the
important end of the rat.

"I'm going to take another one," she
said. "Close your eyes."

This time her aim was better, but
there was no rat in the doorway.

"Oh no," said Marilla. "It's gone."

"No," I said. "It's not gone. I think
it's sniffing my shoe."

I stood up quick and Marilla and
Dave jumped back. Dave turned on his
watch light and tried to shine it on my
feet. It was hard to see, but there it
was--with two paws on my shoe.

If you think it's silly to be scared
of a rat, then you've never had a rat
standing on your shoe before. It was a
lot bigger than I thought a rat was.
Heavy. It looked big enough that it
could really hurt you if it decided to.

It was too dark to tell for sure, but it did seem to have a human face.

I could see its eyes gleaming, and something else. Teeth?

"Don't move, Lyle," said Marilla. "Let me get a picture."

Her camera beeped but there was no flash.

"Oh shoot, hold on a second," she said.

"Hurry!"

"The flash has to charge up."

"Don't let it bite you, Lyle," said Dave. "I read on the Internet that rats carry the plague."

My heart was beating faster and faster. Dave's watch light went out again and for just a half second it was unbelievably dark and scary! Then the light came back on. The rat hadn't moved yet. I could see the tiniest little glitters coming from its eyes. It was watching me.

Frankly, that seems like something we should have discussed before entering the rat's lair!

I felt it put all its weight on my shoe and sniff my pant leg.

"Hurry up, Marilla," I said.

"The batteries are getting weak," she said. "I don't think the flash is going to work. Oh wait, there it goes."

Then I felt its claws grabbing at my pants.

"It's climbing up my leg! Take the picture!"

Suddenly, Dave shouted, "RODENTIA ADVENCHA!"

He almost scared me to death. I jumped and that made the rat panic. But instead of running away it ran right up me! I felt it go up my leg and then cling to my sweater.

Dave said later that I made a squeal. He's probably right. It's a natural reaction to make a squeal when a rat's clawing your stomach!

"Are you crazy?" Marilla hissed at Dave.

"No, I'm the Rhyme-jitsu master!" said Dave. "Rodentia is the scientific name for the rodent family. <u>Adventure</u>, pronounced with a slight accent— ad-ven-cha—is what Lyle is having right now with a rodentia."

"Just take the picture!" I begged.

"First-ever three-syllable Rhyme-jitsu," said Dave. "Five points. HYAH!"

Dave's <u>hyah</u> must have pushed the Rat with the Human Face too far. It let out a wild noise and lunged right at my head!

I screamed, and the room lit up again with the camera flash and I saw the rat's human face for one tiny second before the room went dark again and the rat landed on <u>my</u> face.

SECTION XVII
Really Up Close

I'll go ahead and tell you that
the picture stinks so that you're not
expecting to see a photograph of the
Rat with the Human Face crawling on
my face. The photo just looks like a
blurry fuzz ball or something.

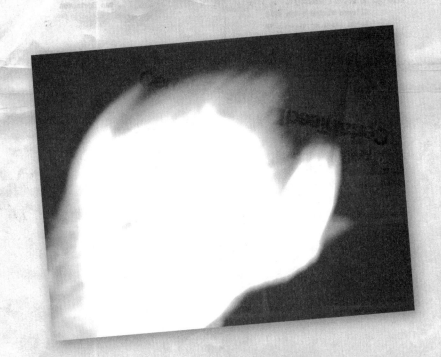

   That's not what I saw, and Marilla
and Dave say so too. It just doesn't
capture the ratness or the humanness.
Dave tried to draw a picture of what
we saw.

   As you can see, the rat in Dave's
picture looks a lot like George
Washington. It's true. It DID! I'm

not one hundred percent sure I would
say it had a human face. But for a
rat it looked an awful lot like George
Washington.

Marilla said it looked like Elvis,
but I got a lot better look at it than
she did and I know what I saw when
that flash went off, and it was a George
Washington rat all lit up with his
mouth wide open and all these teeth and
it was screaming this awful sound kind
of like . . . like nothing else, because
only the Rat with the Human Face can
sound like that.

Marilla and Dave both screamed too
but I was the loudest, because I realized
that if it was lunging at my face, it was
going to land on my face and probably
eat it.

But it didn't. It used me like a
launchpad. It dug its claws into my nose
and my cheek and just sprang off into
the darkness. I felt the claws and this
huge furry weight--five pounds?--and
last of all this long fleshy tail.

UNOFFICIAL Personal Note

So why didn't it eat me? Well, here's something I haven't told Dave or Marilla. During that tiny second that the flash went off, our eyes met. Mine and the rat's, I mean. They weren't beady like rat eyes are supposed to be. They were scared but also kind of wise and friendly. Like George Washington's eyes probably were. I think the rat knew I wasn't going to hurt it so it just jumped off and disappeared.

We never heard it land anywhere or run off or anything. Dave shined his light all around but we saw nothing. I asked him to shine it on my face to see if I was bleeding.

That's when the basement door banged open.

"WHAT THE $@&* is going on down here?"

SECTION XVIII
Big Trouble

You might think that having a rat climb all over your face would be the worst thing that could happen to you.

No, that's not even close. In fact, the rat part was actually exciting and I try to remember it now as being worth all the trouble we got into.

The minute the caretaker opened the door, that's when things started to go really, really bad. It was the end of our adventure and the end of The Qwikpick Adventure Society.

Now that I've had time to think about it, I don't think he was a bad guy or anything. I can see why he was so mad, finding a bunch of kids messing around in the basement.

But he wasn't half as mad as Terri was.

See, the caretaker, whose name we never even found out, asked us how we got there and what we were doing and all that.

Then he said he should call the police but instead he would take us back to Terri at the hotel.

He loaded us into the old pickup truck we had seen—it only looked broken down—and took us up there and dragged us into the dining room, where Terri and the old ladies were eating dessert.

He told Terri where he found us and how we had snuck in and could have been locked in for weeks if he hadn't heard me screaming.

All that would have been bad enough, but then just before he left he made a comment about "people bringing $@*&@$ kids up on the $@*(&@ mountain and letting them run wild." Except he said it like "rrrrhunn wiiild."

And he said that right in front of all the ladies and whoever else was in the dining room, which was packed.

Then he left, and Terri was about to erupt when one of the old ladies said, "What's on their shoes?"

We all looked down and Terri looked down and prob ably everybody in the hotel looked down and saw that there was all this nasty black stuff on our shoes and on the carpet.

Marilla, Dave, and I all knew what it was. It was rat poop. The basement must have been full of it. But we didn't tell Terri what it was, obviously.

Anyway, she was still about to erupt, but she marched us back out to the bus first. On my way out I got a look at the buffet. It didn't look like the buffet at Kountry Korner. It looked like one of those feasts that Middle Ages kings ate where stuff is piled up on silver platters. It looked like the greatest meal anybody ever had. There was even an ice sculpture of an eagle.

When we got on the bus, Terri had her eruption. She went berserk. She looked crazier than the rat. And possibly less human.

I can't even tell you exactly what she said. But it was a long stream of things like "I can't believe" and

"Do you have any idea?" and "You're my responsibility" and "I don't need this @#$*" and "When I tell your parents."

One of the big problems was exactly what Terri was going to tell our parents. She was making every little bit of it sound worse than what it was. She kept saying we had lied to her face. But that was a lie itself, because we had been careful not to actually tell her any lies.

The bigger problem was how what we had actually done kept being described with new words. When we started, we said we were "exploring." Even the caretaker had just called it "sneaking in."

But Terri kept saying "breaking in," which sounded like an actual crime. I thought about correcting her and telling her that the door wasn't locked and we hadn't broken anything, but I was scared to say it.

I knew that if she said "breaking in" to our parents, especially Marilla's parents, it was going to be really bad.

I may as well point out that while listening to Terri I finally realized that I had a big wet spot on my pants, down near my knee. That rat must have peed on me! I hope you can't get the plague from rat pee.

We were doomed and we knew it. But even Marilla, who was crying the hardest this whole time, didn't know just how doomed we were.

Finally, Marilla was crying so hard that Terri stopped and went back into the hotel to get the old ladies.

None of us had said anything to each other since the caretaker. We hadn't had a chance. We'd had somebody yelling at us the whole time.

"Guys, I'm sorry. If I hadn't screamed like that, we wouldn't have got caught and we might have found another way out."

"True," said Dave.

"Oh, come on, Dave," yelled Marilla, "you screamed too. And if you hadn't been going 'Hyah!' you wouldn't have scared the rat so bad."

"Oh yeah, that reminds me," said Dave. "That five points puts me totally in the lead. Marilla, let me see the score book."

"Just shove it, Dave!" shouted Marilla.

"I just wanted to write it down before I forgot," whispered Dave.

UNOFFICIAL Personal Note

Wow, this was really bad. Dave and I have occasionally told each other to shove it or to shut up or whatever, but Marilla never says anything like that. I think it finally made Dave realize that this was a super-huge deal for Marilla. She was going to be in a lot more trouble than either of us.

Personally, I was glad that neither of them had blamed me for having pushed them to ignore the no trespassing sign. I still don't think it was me. I think it was the $120 that really made us do it. Of course, I really did want to see that rat, and in a way I'm glad I did. But I sure wish it hadn't destroyed The Qwikpick Adventure Society.

About this time, the cigarette-butt-picker-upper guy stuck his head in the bus door.

"Heard you guys got in trouble for tracking some kind of crap in on the rug. Don't sweat it. People smear stuff on that carpet all the time. I got a special machine to get it out."

"I'm really sorry," I said. "We didn't know we had stepped in it."

"Like I said, no problem, dudes. One of those old ladies dropped a bowl of strawberry goop on the floor, so I was going to have to get out the machine anyway. All right, good rapping with ya. Be good." And he disappeared.

That made me and Dave feel a lot better, but I don't think it did much for Marilla.

The old ladies came back a minute after that and they were all staring at us while they took their seats. And they weren't cha ttering so much and Terri wasn't joking around with them anymore.

"All right," Terri said, "I'm taking the ladies back to the rec center. Then I'm

I gotta say here that I was really starting to hate Terri. Marilla doesn't like it when I say I hate someone, like Jeremy or Mr. Michaels. But some people are jerks, so why should I have to like them?

taking each of you home and I'm going to talk with your parents. Now, just sit there and be quiet!"

It didn't seem like it took as long to get back to Crickenburg as it had taken to get to the lake that morning.

Later, Dave told me he spent the whole trip trying to think of some way out or something he could say to Terri. So did I, but neither of us thought of anything.

At that point we were each just thinking about how much trouble we'd be in individually and what punishment we might have, like being grounded or not getting to watch TV or something.

That wouldn't have been so bad. It might have been worth it if I only lost TV. After all, I can only watch one channel anyway.

SECTION XIX
More Trouble

Finally, we got back to the rec center and the ladies got off the bus and they all looked at us again. The nice lady who had maybe been a teacher gave me a smile. It was nice that somebody didn't think we were bad kids.

Then Terri had us tell her where we lived. She drove over to Dave's house first. She told me and Marilla to wait in the bus and not to budge.

"I'm sorry for what I said, Dave," whispered Marilla.

"Bye, Dave. Good luck," was all I could think of to say.

UNOFFICIAL Personal Note

His parents would have a freak-out, I was sure. (And I was right.) I noticed a strange car in the driveway. That must have been the cousins who were visiting. It would make his parents especially mad that Dave had gotten in trouble in front of company.

But I wondered if the whole thing wouldn't make his cousins realize he was cooler than they thought, because all they probably did was play video games all day.

Marilla and I were alone at this point. Basically for the last time ever, though I didn't know that then, but I knew it would be the last time for a while.

I really wished I could have thought of something to say to her. But I couldn't tell her it was going to be all right, because I knew it wouldn't be.

Kids who get in trouble all the time have it lucky, because when they get in really big trouble it doesn't seem so bad. But Marilla never ever, ever does anything bad. She never cusses. She totally follows all the Commandments and all that.

So instead of just saying "Oh no, not again," her parents were going to lose their minds. I couldn't even imagine how bad she was going to get it.

Plus, since she never tells a lie, she'd end up having to tell them all kinds of stuff that Terri didn't even know, and she might even end up having to tell her parents about the Fountain of Poop too.

She did.

"Marilla, I really hope you don't get in too much trouble," I said.

"I don't care about getting in trouble," she said.

"What?"

"I deserve it," she said. "I practically lied to my parents to go on the trip. And I went past the no trespassing sign and broke into the laboratory . . ."

"We didn't break into anything," I said.

But that didn't seem to make her feel better.

She was crying pretty hard.

UNOFFICIAL Personal Note

Terri had told us not to budge, but I moved to the seat next to Marilla. I wanted to give her a hug or something, but I was afraid to. So just sitting there was the only thing I could think of to do.

Then I saw Terri coming back.

I knew we only had another couple of seconds together alone. Maybe it wasn't the best time, but I had to ask Marilla about something.

"Marilla, when we were in the basement, were you holding Dave's hand too?"

"Eww. No way," she said, and she actually laughed a tiny little bit even though she was still crying. "I don't like Dave like that."

Then Terri came back and yelled, "I thought I told you not to move!"

But I didn't care, because if Marilla said she didn't like Dave like "that," then she must have also meant that she did like me like "that."

I held her hand for just a second before I went back to my seat.

Then Terri took Marilla to her house and me to my house, but just like I'd told her, my parents were at work. I didn't mention that they worked right next door at the Qwikpick. She asked for my phone number and said she would be calling them that evening.

This made it a lot easier for me. I was able to tell them the whole story first without using the words "breaking in."

When Terri did call, my dad tried to calm her do wn and I could tell he was getting annoyed with her trying to make a big deal about everything. And I heard him say, "Is there evidence that they broke in? According to my son, they simply walked through an unlocked door."

When he hung up the phone, the first thing he said was, "Geez, what a pill."

I'm not trying to say that my parents weren't upset with me, because they were. But they weren't exactly mad. It was more like they were worried about me getting hurt or something.

Dad said he was glad to see that I had enough imagination to do something like that and that if we had just asked him, he would have driven us up there himself--not to go into the basement, but to look around the lake and stuff.

My mom put some stuff that stung on the little scratches the rat had made. She said next time I needed to tell her and Dad exactly where I was going and get their permission first.

And they still gave me an Easter basket full of leftover Easter candy that didn't sell at the Qwikpick. You might think this would stink, but it doesn't. Lots of times it's the expensive stuff that doesn't sell, so I get solid chocolate rabbits, not hollow, and stuff like that.

Dave called me that night to find out how much trouble I got in and to tell me how much he got in. Basically, he's grounded for the rest of the school year. No TV, no PlayStation, and no hanging around at the Qwikpick. That last part is like a punishment for me too!

I was pretty sure that Marilla's parents would make the same no-Qwikpick rule too, and I was right about that, but it turned out that was just the tip of the punishment iceberg. I didn't find out for a while just how bad it was going to be. So let me tell you about something else first.

SECTION XX
The End of The Qwikpick
Adventure Society????

Before going to bed that night, I thought of what I should have said to Marilla on the bus. So I wrote her a note to say she's a good person.

Here's a copy of the note, which I obviously was not going to put in the official report:

Dear Marilla,

   I don't think you should feel like a bad person, because you are not. We just wanted to see something neat and we did and we didn't hurt anything except maybe the hotel carpet and the guy said that was no big deal. I'm glad you are like you are and not like Elizabeth, who didn't want to go. I bet she had a boring day.

   We had an exciting day. In fact, since I found out that you like me it was a _great_ day, because I have liked you for a long time.

                          Your pal,
                          Lyle

I figured I would give her the note
the next day at school. But she didn't
get on the bus the next day. She
didn't come to school and Dave didn't
know what was going on either.

So after school I went over to her
trailer to give it to her. Her father
answered the door--he never gets up to
answer the door, usually--and he said
that I couldn't come to see Marilla
anymore and they didn't want her to
spend time with me at school anymore
either. He didn't yell because he
never seems to have the strength to
yell. He just said it plain. It was
worse than yelling.

I asked him if he would give
Marilla my note, but he said no notes
either. Then he said good-bye and
closed the door.

The next day Marilla didn't get on
the bus either. Her parents drove her
to school. Later, Dave told me that she
and her parents went into the office
to talk to the principal.

She and Dave have the same homeroom and she told him all about her punishment and the meeting with the principal. Then he told me about it in PE while we were waiting to get subbed in for floor hockey. (Never got in!)

Her mother had questioned her and found out all about the rat <u>and</u> the poop fountain <u>and</u> The Qwikpick Adventure Society <u>and</u> the hand-holding.

The first punishment, as I expected, was that she couldn't hang out at the Qwikpick anymore.

The second was that she couldn't spend any time with me anymore because I was clearly a "bad kid." Not just at the Qwikpick, but at school too. I hadn't expected <u>that</u>! (Apparently, Dave is not a "bad kid" and she's still allowed to be friends with him.)

The third punishment was that she couldn't play in the Spring Concert, which I thought was really, really mean.

"They told the principal about the three rules too," Dave said. "And when they told him about you he told them about the time you called Jeremy a pervert. Marilla said he made you sound awful. Then he promised her parents he would check and make sure that you don't eat lunch with us anymore."

So that was the final whammy for me.

No Dave or Marilla at lunch. No Dave or Marilla at the Qwikpick. My punishment ended up being worse than Dave's or Marilla's, because they still had other people to hang around with. For me, it was like the old days when I didn't have any friends.

My brain was ov erloaded with all this, but I was also thinking about something else. Dave had just told me that Marilla had told him that she had told her parents about the hand-holding. So why wasn't Dave brokenhearted and angry?

"Are you mad at me because Marilla and I held hands?" I asked him.

"Why would I be mad?" he said.

"Don't you like her too?" I asked.

"Eww, no way," he said. Then he whispered, "I like somebody else, anyway."

So I gave Dave my note to give to Marilla. And he gave me one back from Marilla while we were waiting in the lunch line.

The somebody else turned out to be Elizabeth. That's why he wanted to invite her on the trip! It all makes sense now! It turned out that my long competition with Dave over Marilla didn't really exist. I was extra-glad because if Dave had been mad at me for that, then I really wouldn't have had anybody to talk to at all.

Dear Lyle,

You are my best friend in the whole world. I had to promise my parents not to be your friend anymore, but that was a lie and I'm not sorry for it because I can't help it. I've asked Jesus to forgive me for the lie, but I don't think I need to ask him to forgive me for liking you because that is not a bad thing.

I'm not going to get to see you much anymore, but I will still be your friend even if my parents make us move out of the trailer park like they're talking about.

I also had to promise not to be part of The Qwikpick

Adventure Society anymore. So maybe it is bad for me to give you this. It's the card from my camera. Luckily, my parents didn't ask about it or they probably would have taken it. But I want you to take it to Walgreens and print out the rat pictures for the report.

I'd like to write you a million letters, but I promised not to send you notes either, so even this note is a sin. So I can't write anymore.

I miss you!

Love,
Marilla

When I saw the word <u>love</u> I almost fell down. It made me feel great even if other parts of the note were major-league bad news.

When I read over the report, I realize I have complained a lot about Dave, mostly because he can be bossy. But he's also a really great best friend and fun to do stuff with and not a jerk like most of the other guys in school. And I can't wait until his punishment time is over so he can come over to the Qwikpick again.

And then came the really painful part. Dave and I got to the end of the lunch line and got our trays, and then there was nothing for me to do but try to find a new place to sit.

"Want me to sit with you?" asked Dave.

I looked over at the nerd table and Marilla was sitting there with no lunch and she looked totally miserable.

"You better go sit with Marilla," I said. "Besides, Elizabeth would miss you too much."

"Shut up," said Dave, but he was smiling. He went over to the nerd table.

They were talking and goofing around and being stupid like usual and I knew there was no other place

in the whole cafeteria that would be
nearly as much fun.

Of course, they were probably talking
about the Spring Concert and that made me
feel bad for Marilla because now she was
left out of it, just like I was, and she
would have to hear all about it and even
learn the songs for it in class but not
get to go.

I tried to smile at her, but she was
just staring at her lunch.

Then I saw the principal wandering
around and decided to find a seat before
he had a chance to come over and say
anything.

Every empty seat was saved, of course,
until I finally found a seat that no one
else wanted. Right next to Carrie Felman.
Great.

• • •

By the way, the final score for Rhyme-
jitsu was Lyle (me) 131, Marilla 142, Dave
145. That's right--he won because of that
stupid "rodentia advencha" rhyme, which
turned out to be the last Rhyme-jitsu
rhyme ever.

I got Dave to give it to Marilla.
Maybe it will cheer her up some.

The next time I went to the Qwikpick break room--all by myself, of course--guess who was there? Andrew Jackson. It turned out that Larry had tried to buy him from the crane game guy for us. But the crane game guy said that he could have him for free because they were replacing all the Andrew Jacksons with Batmans.

I wish I could tell you what happened to the Rat with the Human Face. I kind of worry that the caretaker put out traps to kill him. But that rat seemed pretty smart so I don't think he'll get caught by a trap. I mean, George Washington wouldn't get caught in a rat trap, would he?

And that's it, except that one day Marilla gave Dave a poem she had written and he gave it to me. I think it's really good.

Ode to the Rat with the Human Face

You have a very
pretty smile.
I'm glad you didn't
bite my friend Lyle.

You climbed all the
way up his leg.
I hope that he
doesn't get the plague.

Some might say your
smell is a curse,
but that's okay,
we've smelled worse.

I hope you are not
lonely in your dark
place.
I hope there's
another rat with a
human face.

We, the undersigned, swear that this is the true story of the now banned Qwikpick Adventure Society's Expedition to Find the Rat with the Human Face.

Lyle Hertzog

Marilla Anderson

David H. Raskin

UNOFFICIAL Personal Note

And I, Lyle Hertzog, co-founder and recording secretary of The Qwikpick Adventure Society, swear, or at least hope, that somehow I will figure out a way to have another adventure. I just have to come up with something so good that Marilla and Dave will be willing to break the rules to do it. I haven't thought of it yet but I'm working on it.

Got it!

Tom Angleberger is the author of the <u>New York Times</u> bestselling Origami Yoda series. He is also the author of <u>Fake Mustache</u> and <u>Horton Halfpott</u>, both Edgar Award nominees, and <u>Poop Fountain!</u>, the first book in the Qwikpick Papers series. He has worked as a journalist and lives in the Appalachian Mountains of Virginia with his wife. Visit him online at www.origamiyoda.com.

COLLECT THEM ALL!

READ ALL OF THE BOOKS IN TOM ANGLEBERGER'S BESTSELLING ORIGAMI YODA SERIES.

SEND AUTHOR FAN MAIL TO:
Amulet Books, Attn: Marketing, 115 West 18th Street, New York, NY 10011.
Or e-mail marketing@abramsbooks.com. All mail will be forwarded.

www.origamiyoda.com

ALSO BY TOM ANGLEBERGER

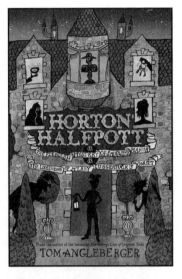

Fake Mustache: *Or, How Jodie O'Rodeo and her Wonder Horse (and Some Nerdy Kid) Saved the U.S. Presidential Election from a Mad Genius Criminal Mastermind*

Horton Halfpot: *Or, The Fiendish Mystery of Smugwick Manor; Or, The Loosening of M'Lady Luggertuck's Corset*

SEND AUTHOR FAN MAIL TO:
Amulet Books, Attn: Marketing, 115 West 18th Street, New York, NY 10011.
Or e-mail marketing@abramsbooks.com. All mail will be forwarded.

THE QWIKPICK PAPERS

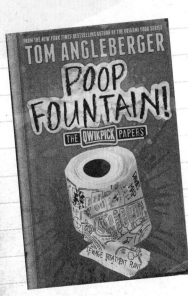

Amulet Books
An imprint of ABRAMS

WWW.AMULETBOOKS.COM